THEY MAKE
GREAT STOCKING
STUFFERS!

Be sure to read **ALL** the **BABYMOUSE** books:

A VERY BABYMOUSE CHRISTMAS

BY JENNIFER L. HOLM & MATTHEW HOLM

RANDOM HOUSE 🏠 NEW YORK

LOOKS LIKE IT'S GOING TO BE A PINK CHRISTMAS!

Copyright © 2011 by Jennifer Holm and Matthew Holm. All rights reserved.
Published in the United States by Random House Children's Books, a division of Random House LLC, a Penguin Random House Company, New York.
Random House and the colophon are registered trademarks of Random House LLC.

Visit us on the Web!
randomhouse.com/kids
Babymouse.com

Educators and librarians, for a variety of teaching tools, visit us at RHTeachersLibrarians.com

Library of Congress Cataloging-in-Publication Data
Holm, Jennifer L.
Babymouse : a very Babymouse Christmas / by Jennifer L. Holm and Matthew Holm. — 1st ed.
   p.   cm.
Summary: A spunky mouse with an active imagination is determined to get the latest electronic gadget for Christmas even if she has to outfox Santa himself to get it.
ISBN 978-0-375-86779-8 (trade) — ISBN 978-0-375-96779-5 (lib. bdg.)
I. Graphic novels. [1. Graphic novels. 2. Christmas—Fiction. 3. Gifts—Fiction. 4. Imagination—Fiction. 5. Mice—Fiction. 6. Animals—Fiction. 7. Humorous stories.]
I. Holm, Matthew. II. Title. III. Title: Very Babymouse Christmas.
PZ7.7.H65 Bac   2011   74L5'973—dc22   2010027988

MANUFACTURED IN MALAYSIA   20 19 18 17 16 15 14 13 12 11 10 9 8 7 6   First Edition

A Visit from St. Nick

By the Narrator

I SAID, "NOT A CREATURE WAS STIRRING, NOT EVEN A **BABYMOUSE**."

THIS IS **MY** CLASSIC.

SANTA!

MOMOMOMOMOMOM!!
COOKIECOOKIECOOKIE!!

BABYMOUSE, I'VE GOT A MILLION THINGS TO DO TO GET READY FOR CHRISTMAS.

AND NO COOKIES, SQUEAK! IT'S ALMOST DINNER!

MAYBE I CAN HELP YOU, BABYMOUSE.

DOES TYRANNOSAURUS REX HAVE TWO S'S OR ONE?

WHAT'S THAT YOU'RE WORKING ON?

I'M WRITING A LETTER TO SANTA TELLING HIM WHAT I WANT FOR CHRISTMAS.

A LETTER TO SANTA? HOW CHARMING.

AH, WE HAD SUCH WONDERFUL FAMILY HOLIDAY TRADITIONS. MOTHER WOULD MAKE PLUM PUDDING WHILE FATHER AND I TRIMMED THE TREE. AFTERWARD, WE'D GO ICE-SKATING AND HAVE HOT COCOA.

SCRITCH SCRATCH

YOU HAVE PARENTS?

OF COURSE I HAVE PARENTS, BABYMOUSE.

Father

Mother

NARRATOR

17

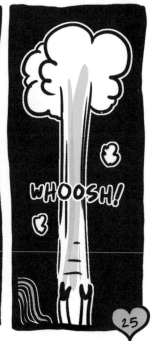

25

LATER.

AND EVEN LATER.

MUCH LATER.

SO VERY MUCH LATER.

I'VE RUN OUT OF WORDS TO DESCRIBE HOW MUCH LATER IT IS.

YOU'RE NEXT!

SCHOOL.

ELEMENTARY SCHOOL

HOLIDAY LOCKER-DECORATING CONTEST

WIN A WHIZ BANG!™

?

HOLIDAY LOCKER-DECORATING CONTEST

WIN A WHIZ BANG!™

COOL!

THE NEXT DAY.

OOF!

NUDGE

I SEE YOU'VE GOT A FEW DECORATIONS, BABYMOUSE.

I'M GOING TO WIN THAT WHIZ BANG™!

FELIZ NAVIDAD

38

"THE DANCE OF THE SUGARPLUM WHIZ BANGS™"!

THIS JUST ISN'T WORKING FOR ME, BABYMOUSE.

YOU HAVE NO TASTE!

51

THE SECOND NIGHT OF HANUKKAH.

DING-DONG!

THIRD NIGHT OF HANUKKAH.

AND THE ONE AFTER THAT.

UH, BABYMOUSE. THAT'S NOT YOUR FAMILY, YOU KNOW.

DING-DONG

BUT IT'S ONLY THE FIFTH DAY! MAYBE THEY WON'T NOTICE ME.

THE DAY OF THE HOLIDAY PARTY AT SCHOOL.

HAPPY HOLIDAYS!

MICE ARE NICE!

AND THIS ONE IS FOR IVAN IGUANA.

SECRET SANTA ↓

AND WILSON THE WEASEL.

AND BETSY BIRD.

A FEW DAYS LATER.

DECEMBER

ONLY TWO DAYS UNTIL I GET MY WHIZ BANG™!

YOU KNOW, BABYMOUSE, CHRISTMAS ISN'T ABOUT PRESENTS. IT'S ABOUT FAMILY AND FRIENDSHIP AND LOVE.

SHAKE

SHAKE

HAVE YOU HEARD OF A LITTLE BOOK CALLED **HOW THE GRINCH STOLE CHRISTMAS!?**

MAYBE THEY SHOULD GIVE IT A NEW TITLE: **THE GREEDY BABYMOUSE WHO WAS TOTALLY OBSESSED WITH GETTING A WHIZ BANG™.**

WORKS FOR ME!

HE DOESN'T LOOK SO "TINY" TO ME.

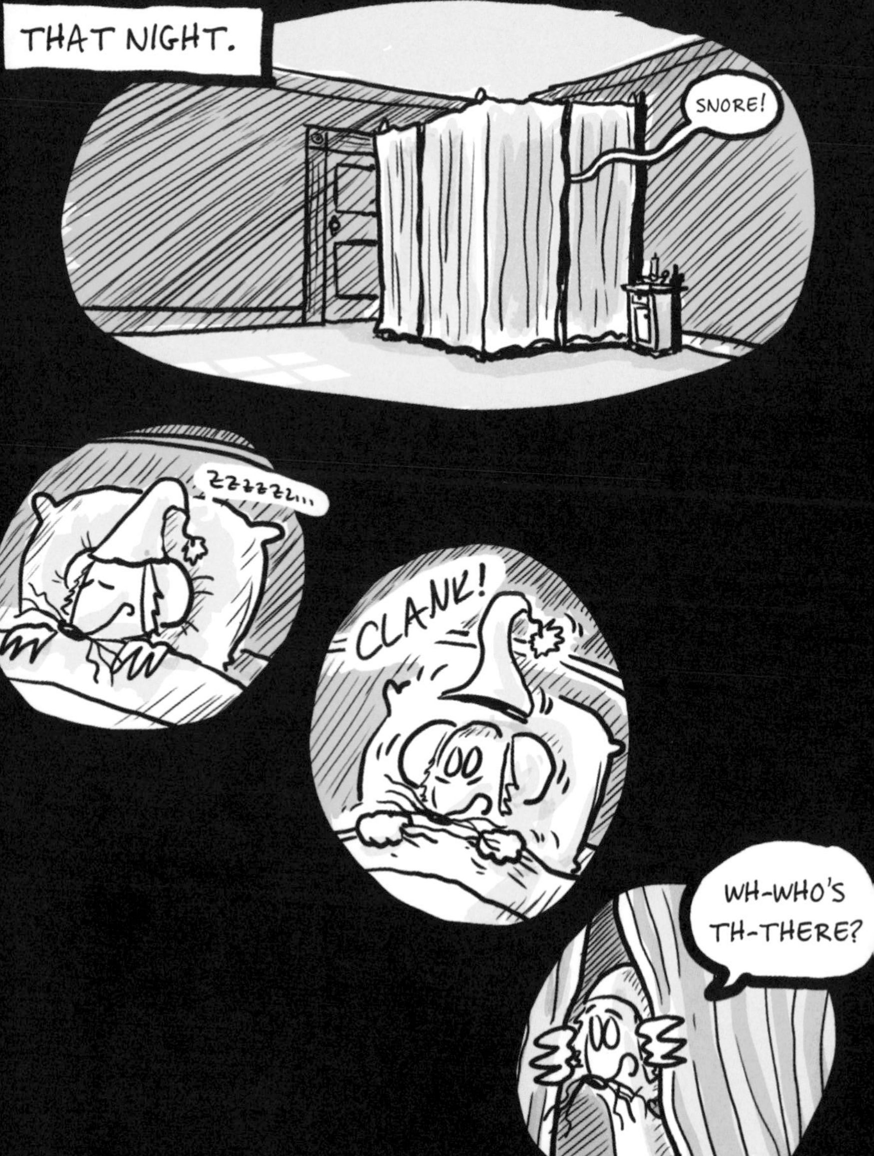
THAT NIGHT.
SNORE!
ZZZZZZZ...
CLANK!
WH-WHO'S TH-THERE?

CLANK!

FLUMP!

WHERE ARE WE?

WE'RE IN THE PAST.

BACK WHEN YOU HAD HOMEWORK.

GASP! SCHOOL!

LOOK!

OOF!

PINCH!

SLAM!

NO MORE, SPIRIT!

BUT WE HAVEN'T EVEN GOTTEN TO FIFTH PERIOD YET.

WHAT AM I SUPPOSED TO LEARN FROM THIS, ANYWAY?

THAT YOU HAVE REALLY MESSY WHISKERS.

AND THIS IS SUPPOSED TO BE A CLASSIC?

YOU'RE GOING TO LOVE **GREAT EXPECTATIONS**, BABYMOUSE.

ONE MINUTE LATER.

TICK!

BURP!

BABYMOUSE! WHAT ABOUT SANTA?

EH, HE'S BUSY TONIGHT. HE'LL NEVER KNOW.

LATER.

I DON'T KNOW IF IT'S BIG ENOUGH, BABYMOUSE.

ME NEITHER!

SO WHAT DID YOU GET FOR YOUR FAMILY, BABYMOUSE?

UM, MY FAMILY?

YOU KNOW—YOUR MOTHER? YOUR FATHER? SQUEAK?

UH...

YOU **DID** GET THEM SOMETHING, DIDN'T YOU?

FWIP!

ZOOM!

SWOOSH!

ZIP!

ZOOM!

SWOOP!

LATER.

I'LL BE YOU, SQUEAK, I'LL BE YOU.

COOKIE! COOKIE!

EVEN LATER.

I WONDER IF THE LITTLE WASHING MACHINE WORKS?

BEEP!

MUCH LATER.

OH, LOOK, THERE'S A MESSY ROOM. THAT MUST BE BABYMOUSE'S.

DAD!

87

HAPPY

HOLIDAYS!

READ ABOUT
SQUISH'S AMAZING ADVENTURES IN:

AND COMING SOON:

★ "IF EVER A NEW SERIES DESERVED TO GO
VIRAL, THIS ONE DOES."
–KIRKUS REVIEWS, STARRED

If you like Babymouse,
you'll love these other great books
by Jennifer L. Holm!

THE BOSTON JANE TRILOGY
EIGHTH GRADE IS MAKING ME SICK
MIDDLE SCHOOL IS WORSE THAN MEATLOAF
OUR ONLY MAY AMELIA
PENNY FROM HEAVEN
TURTLE IN PARADISE

THEY'RE REALLY GOOD! TRUST ME!